T0193630

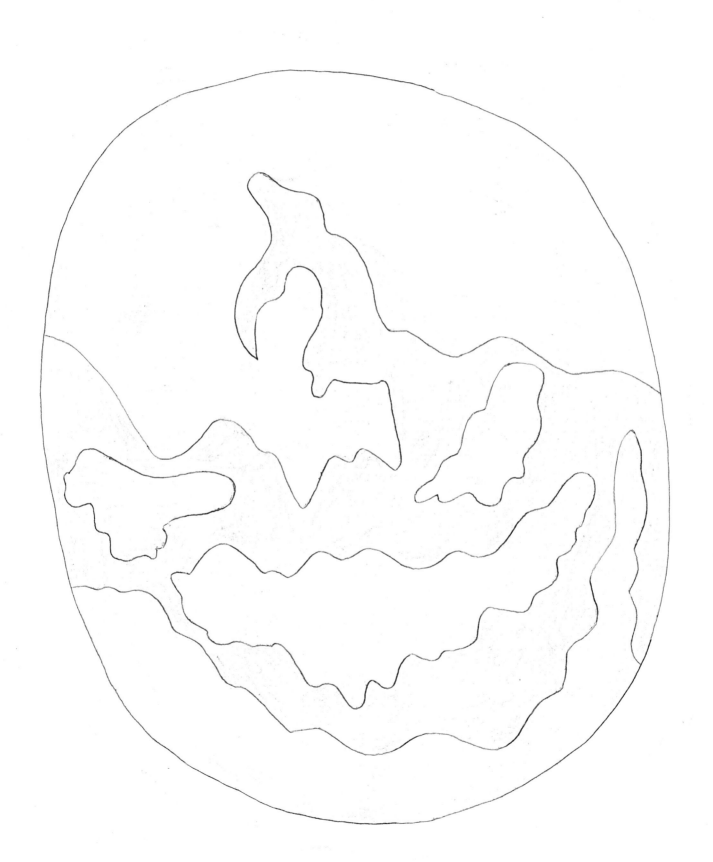

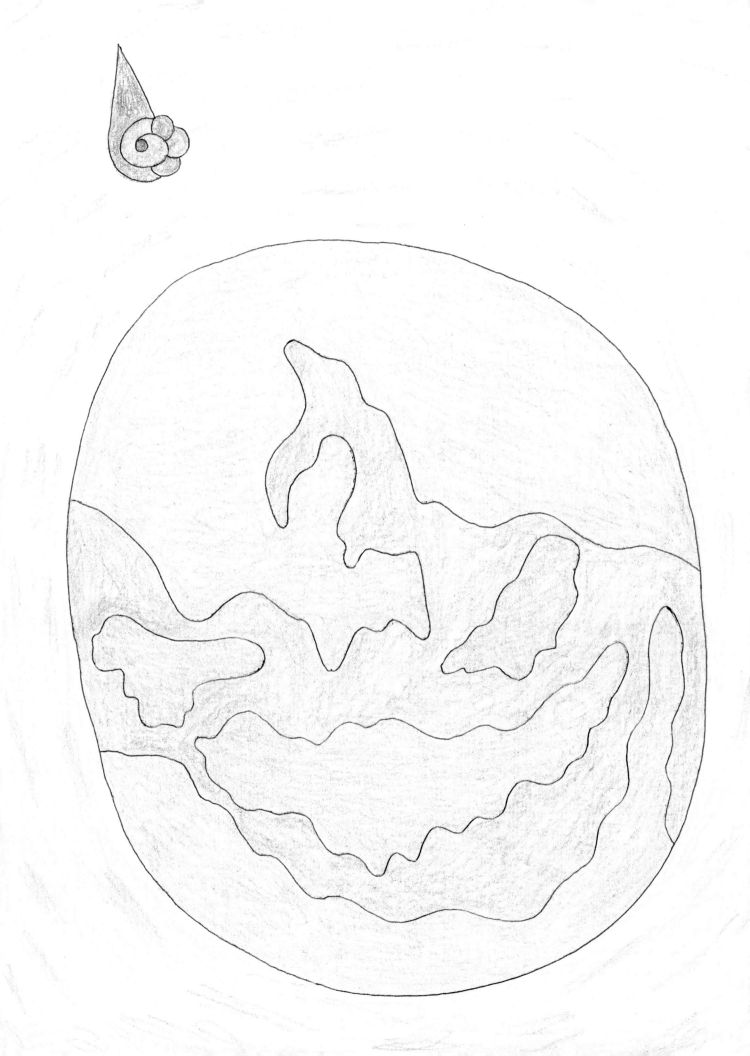

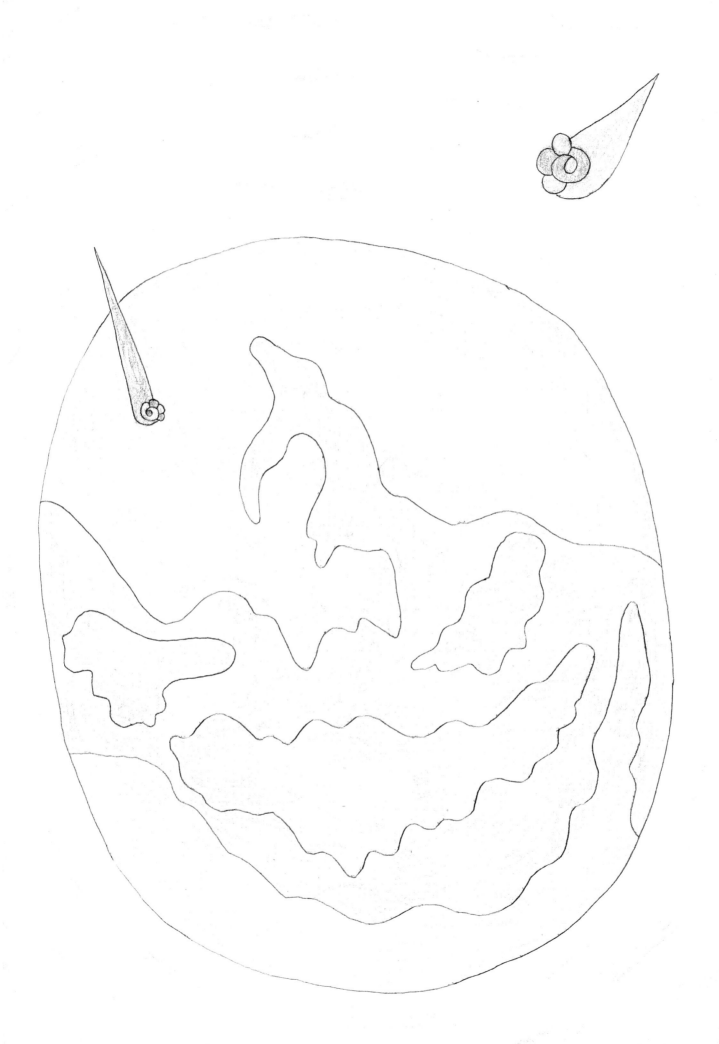

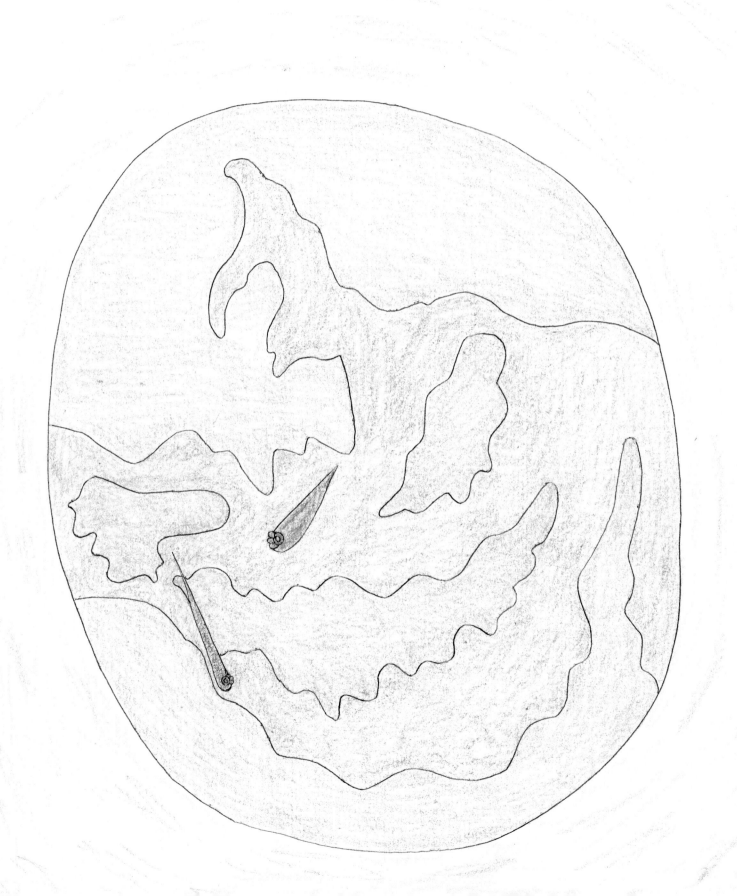

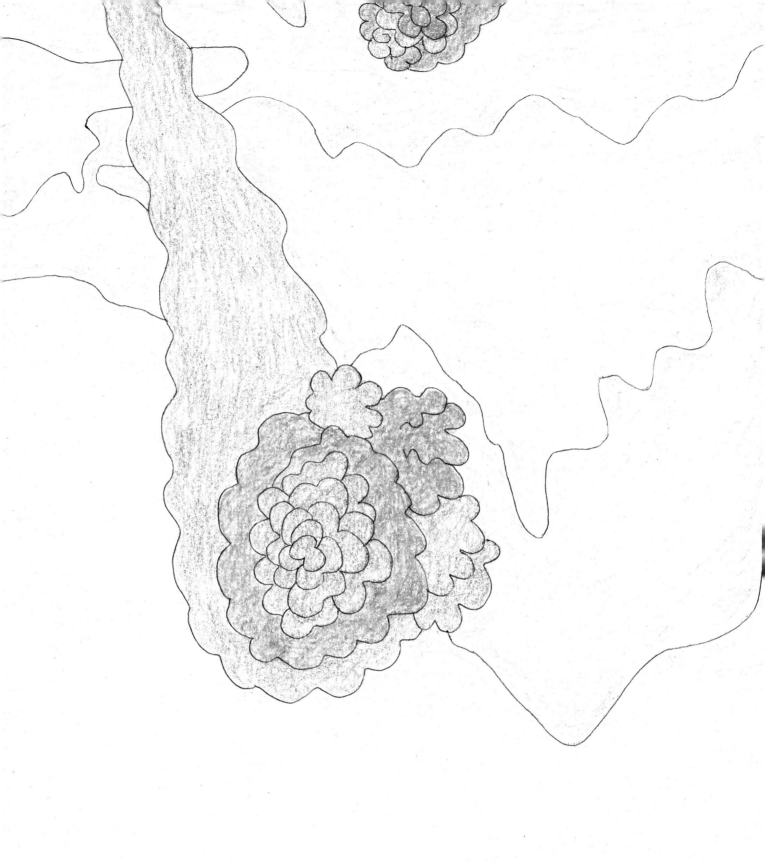

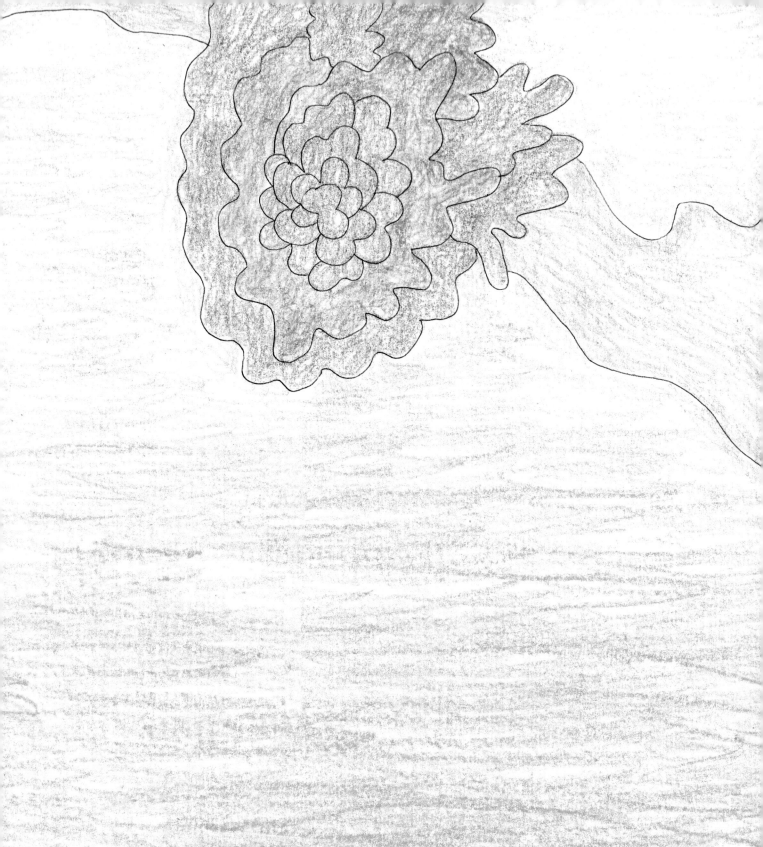

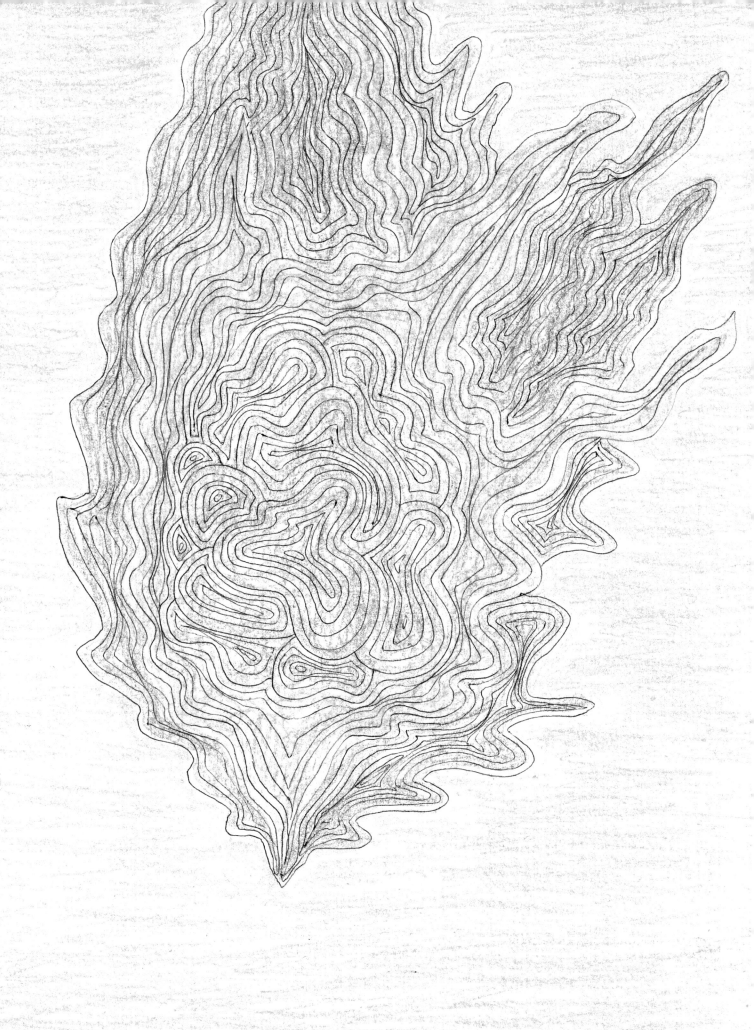

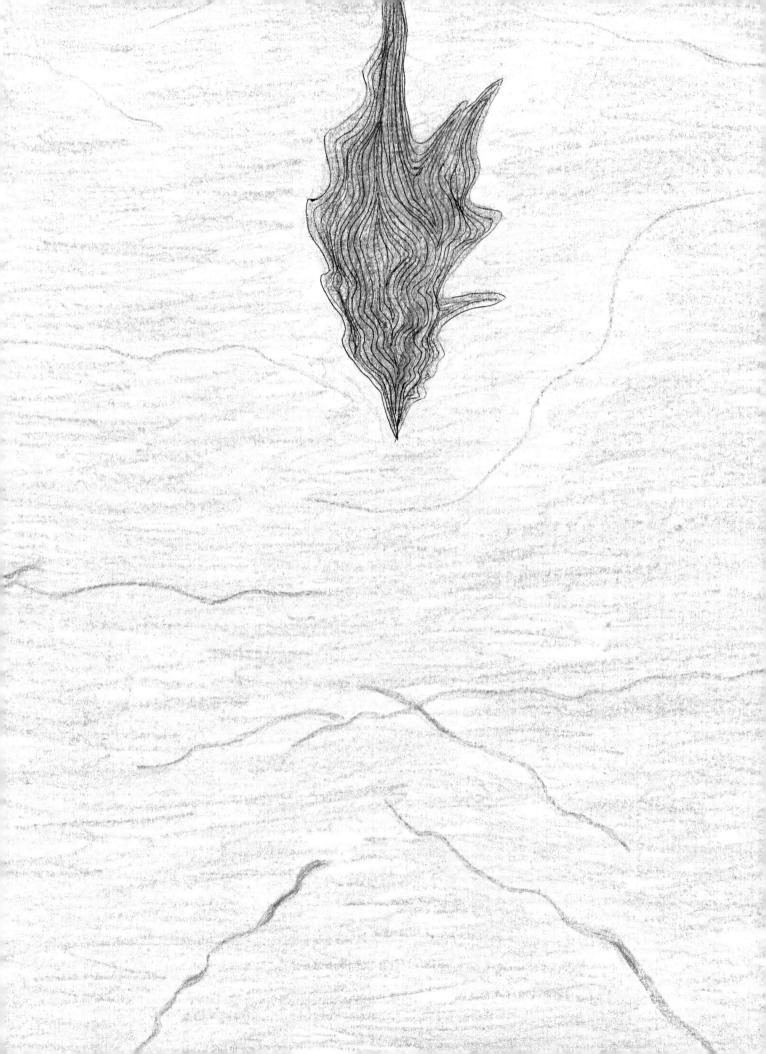

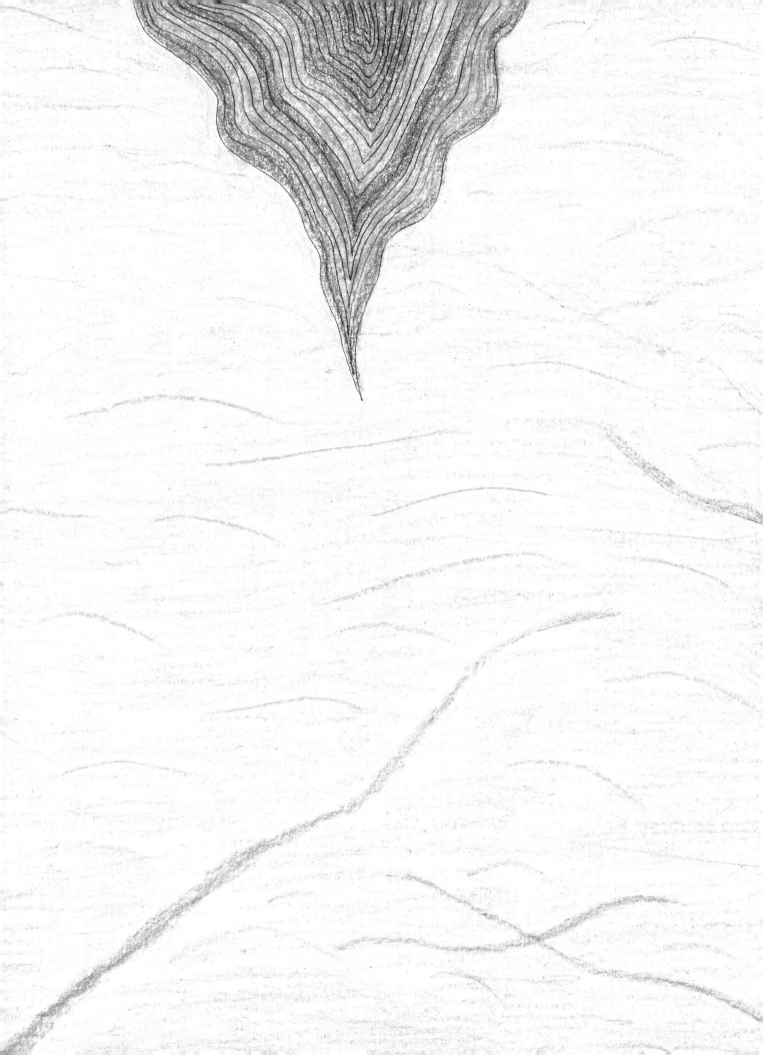

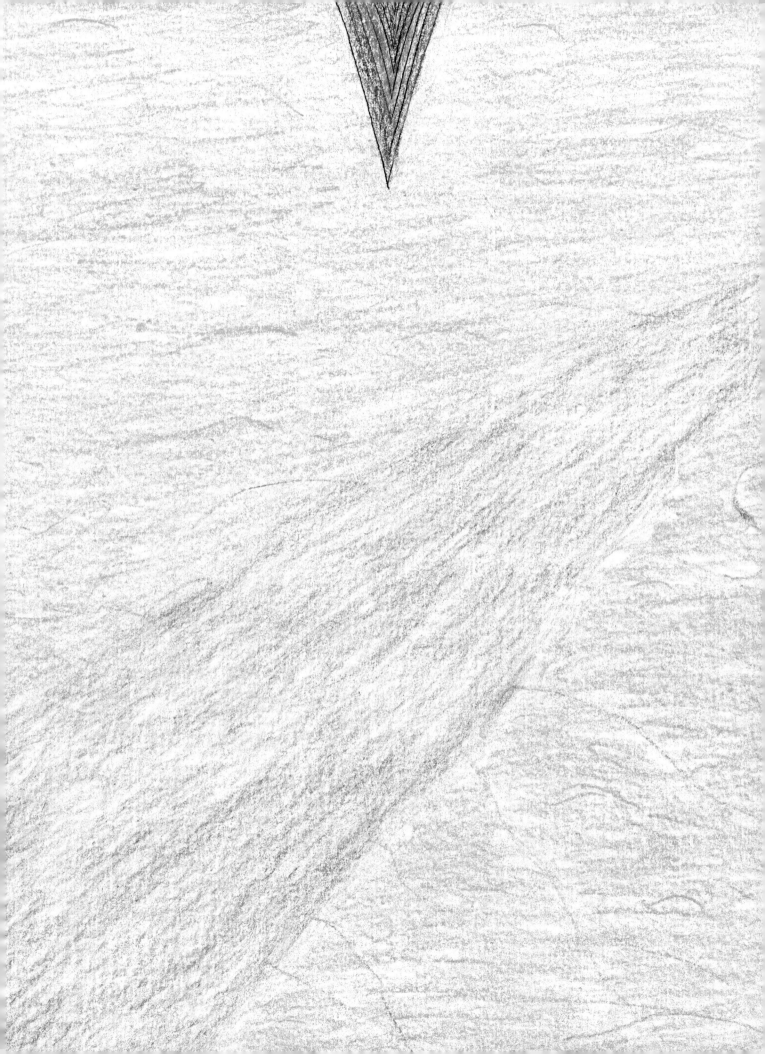

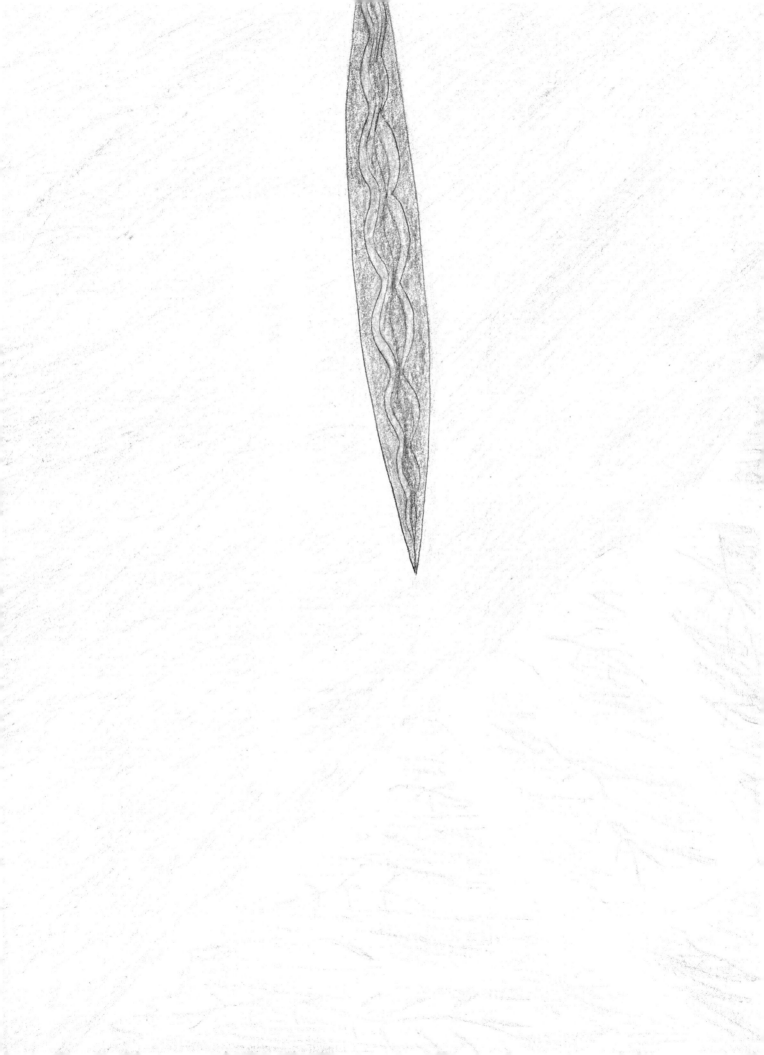

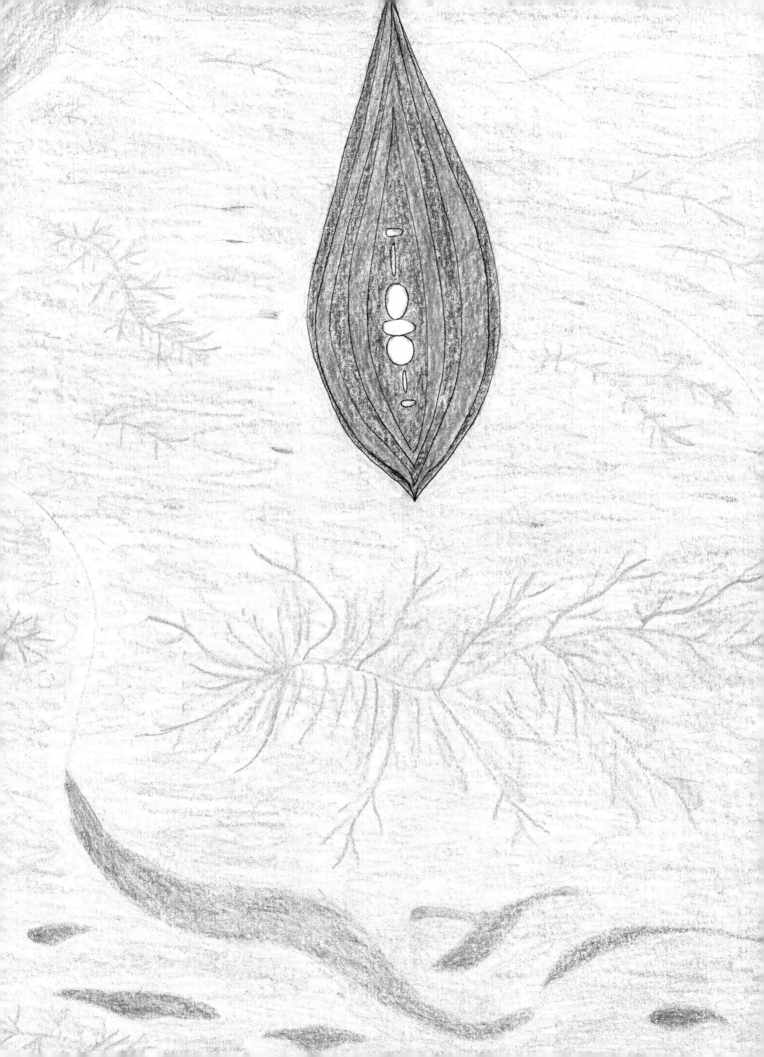

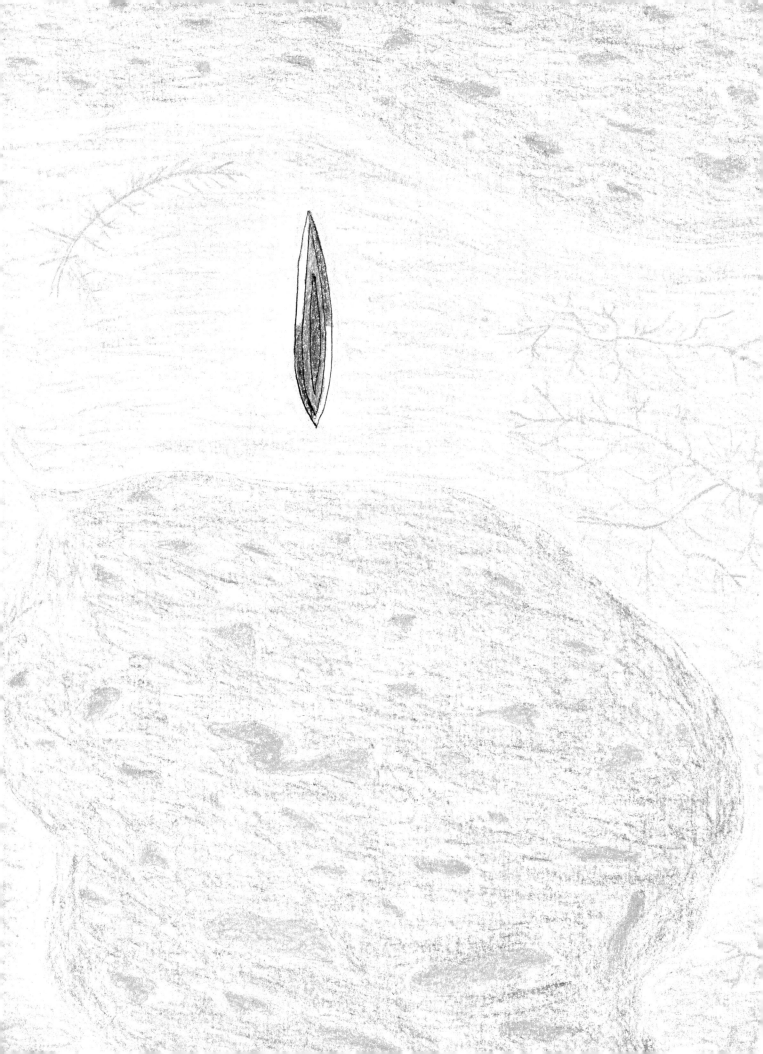

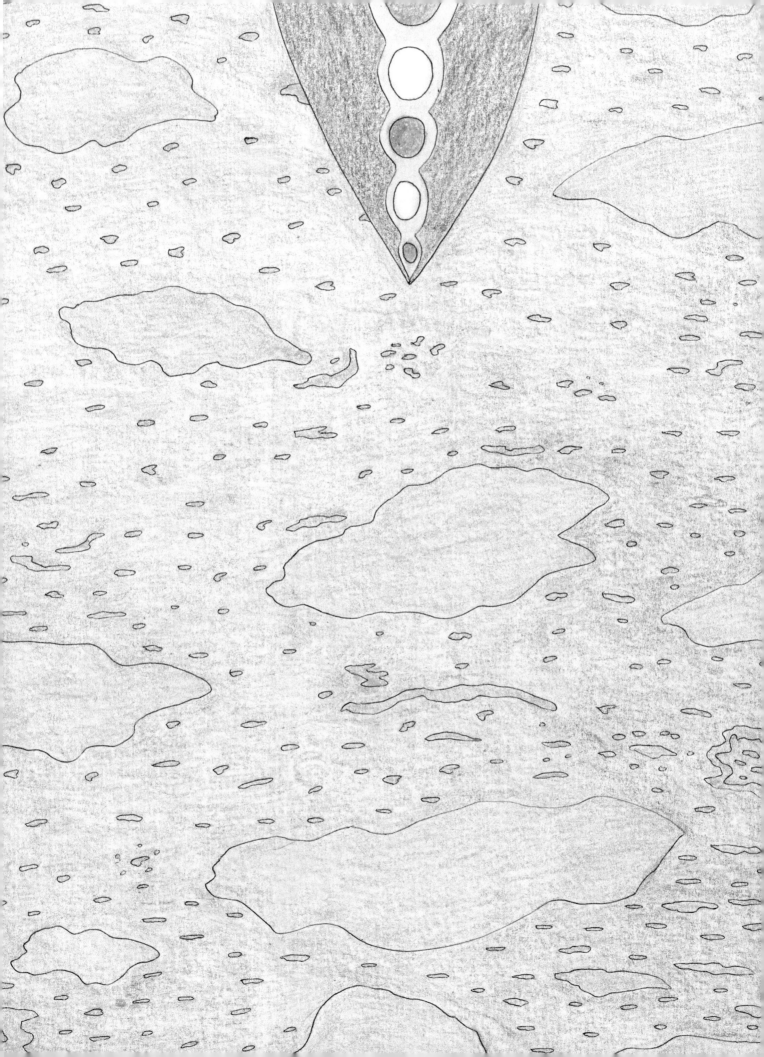

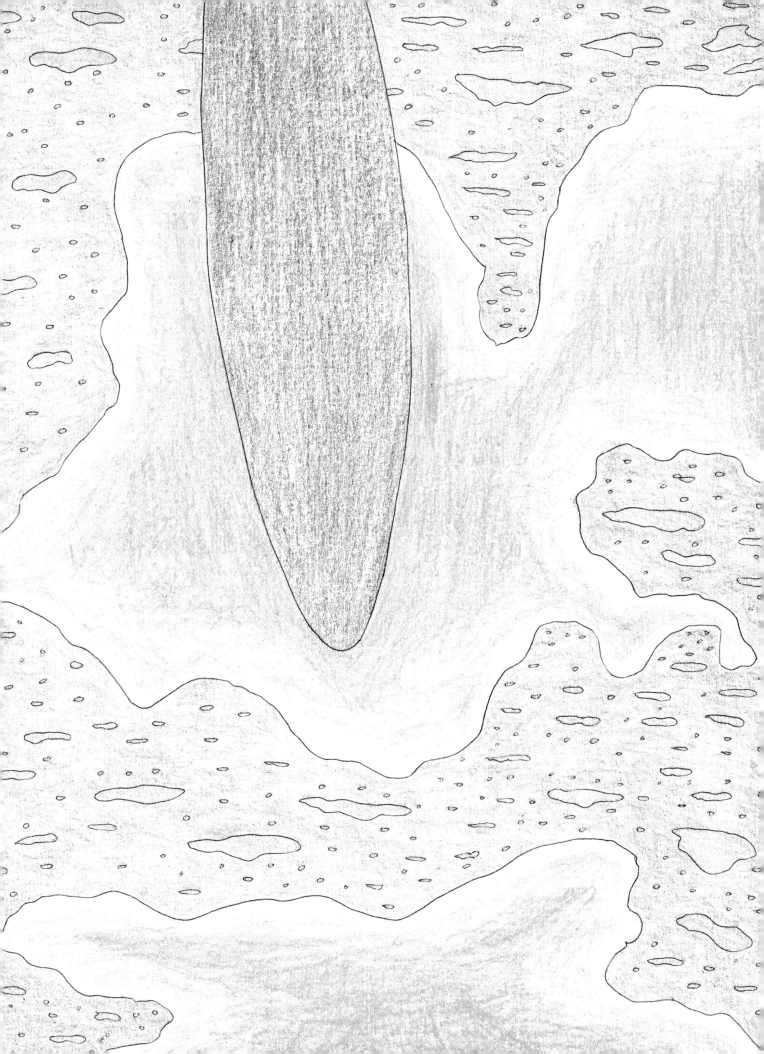

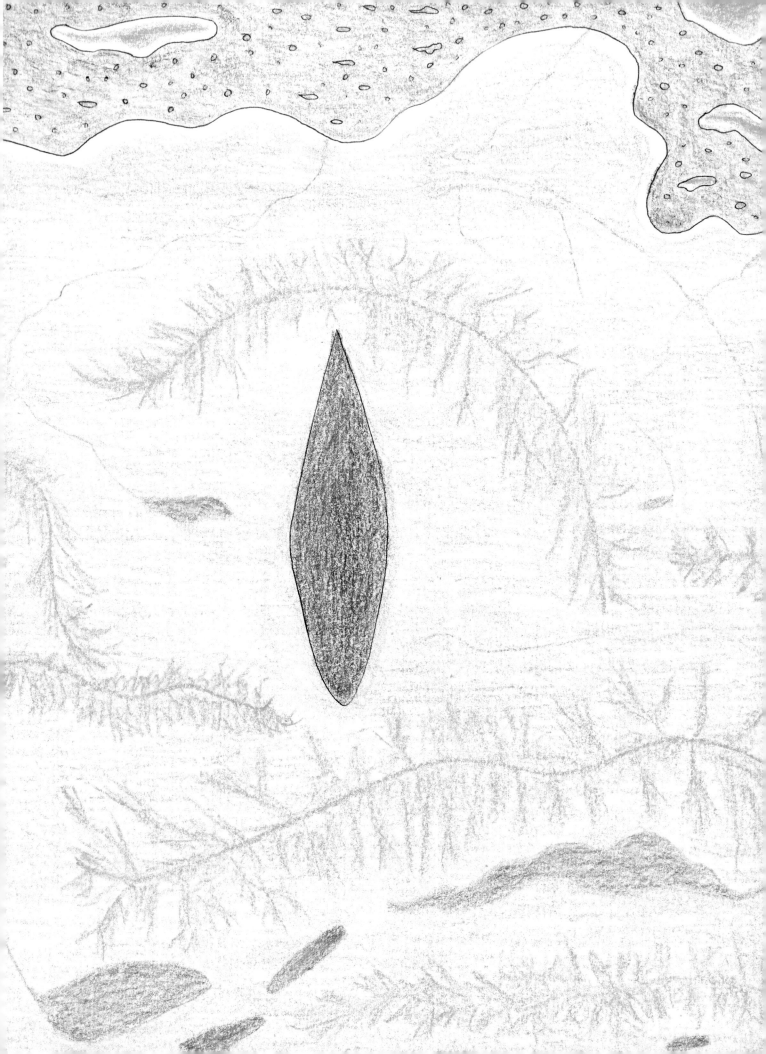

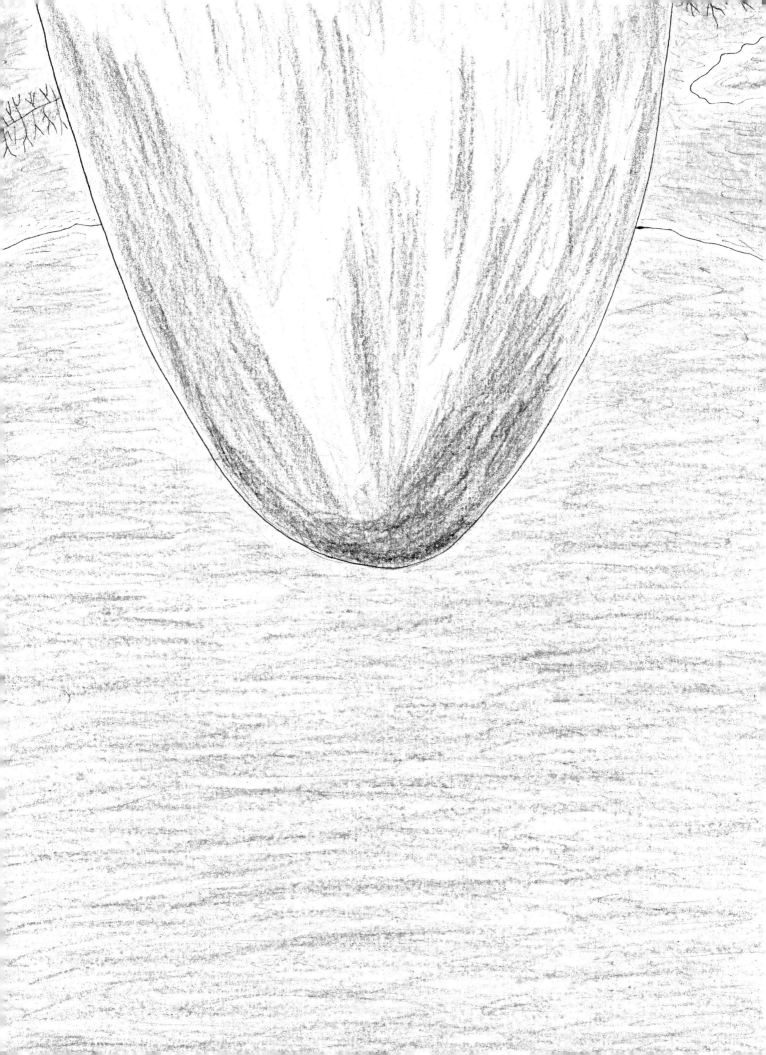

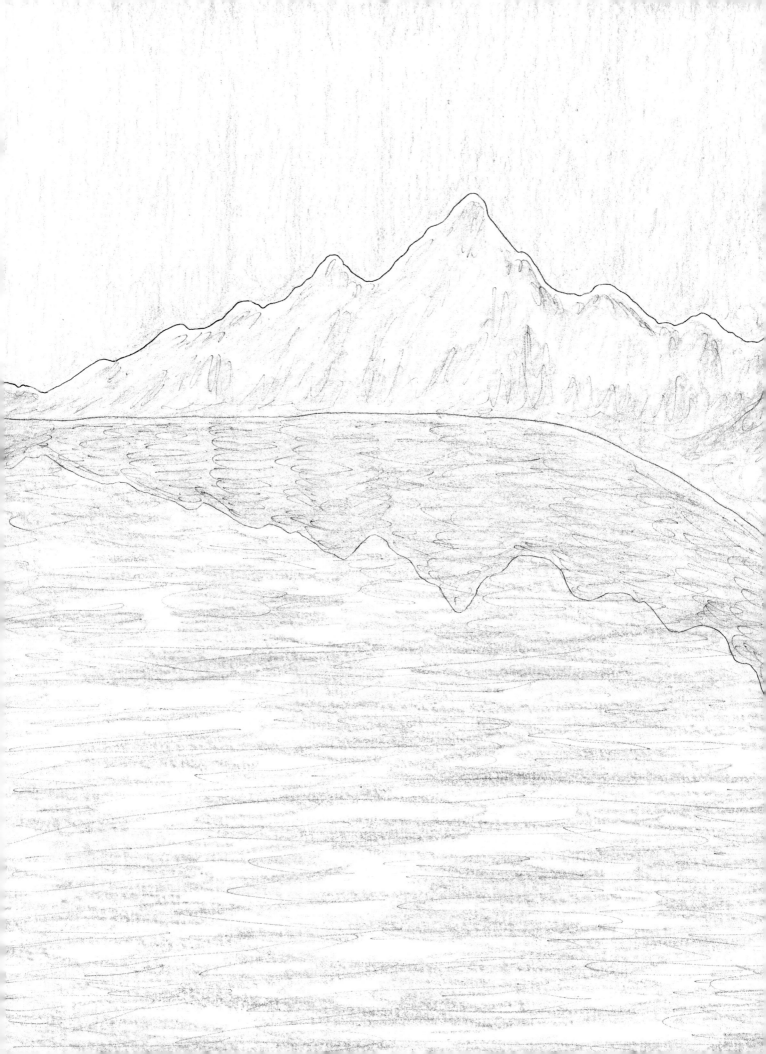

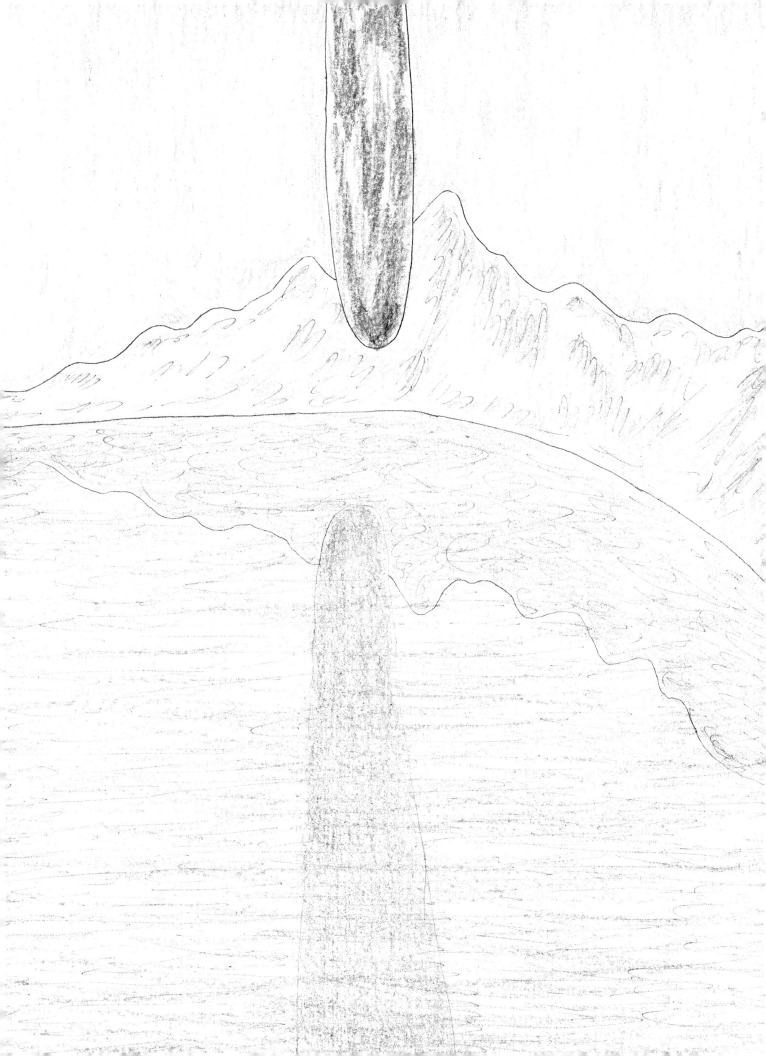

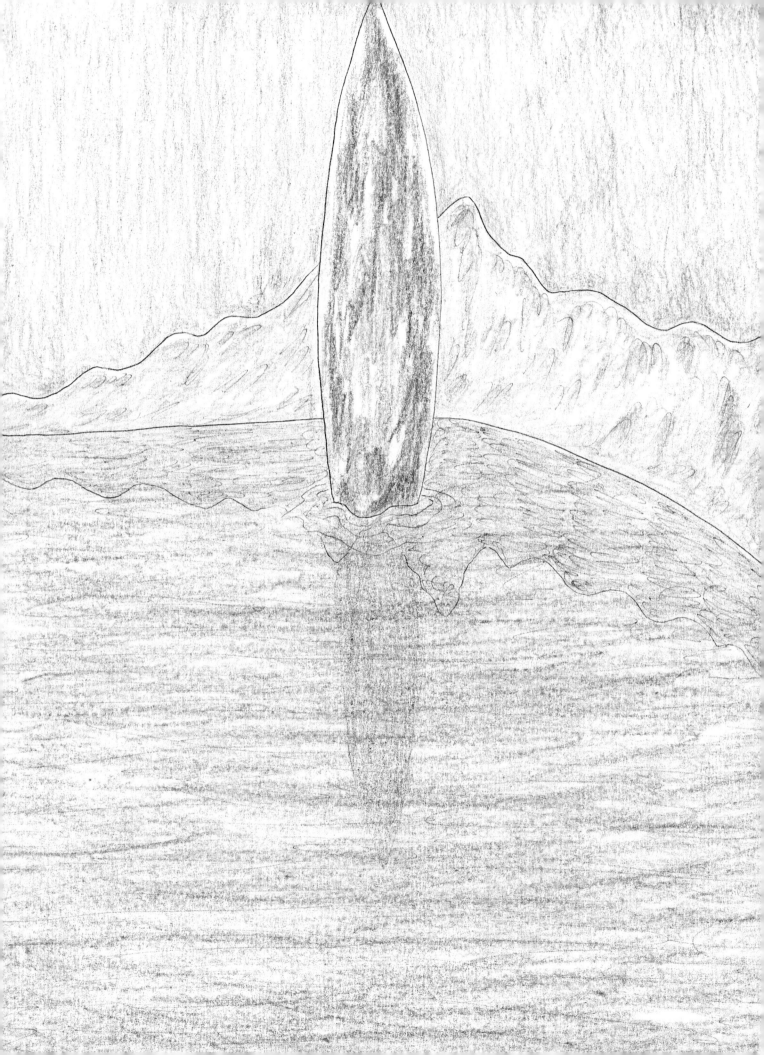

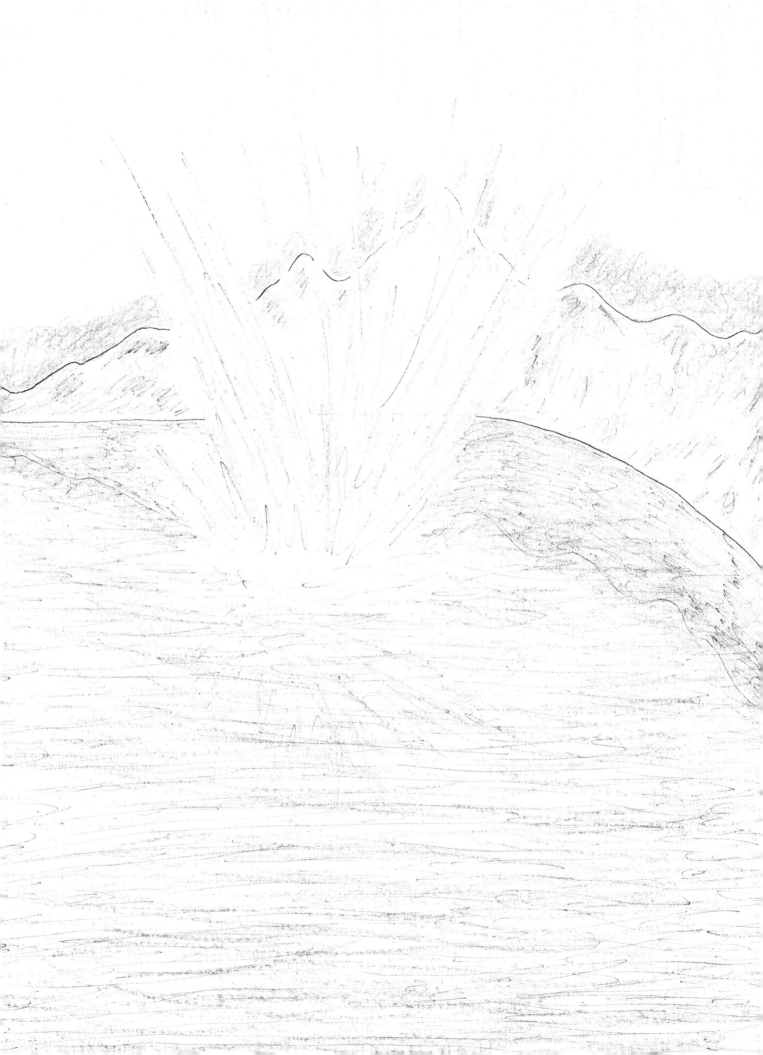

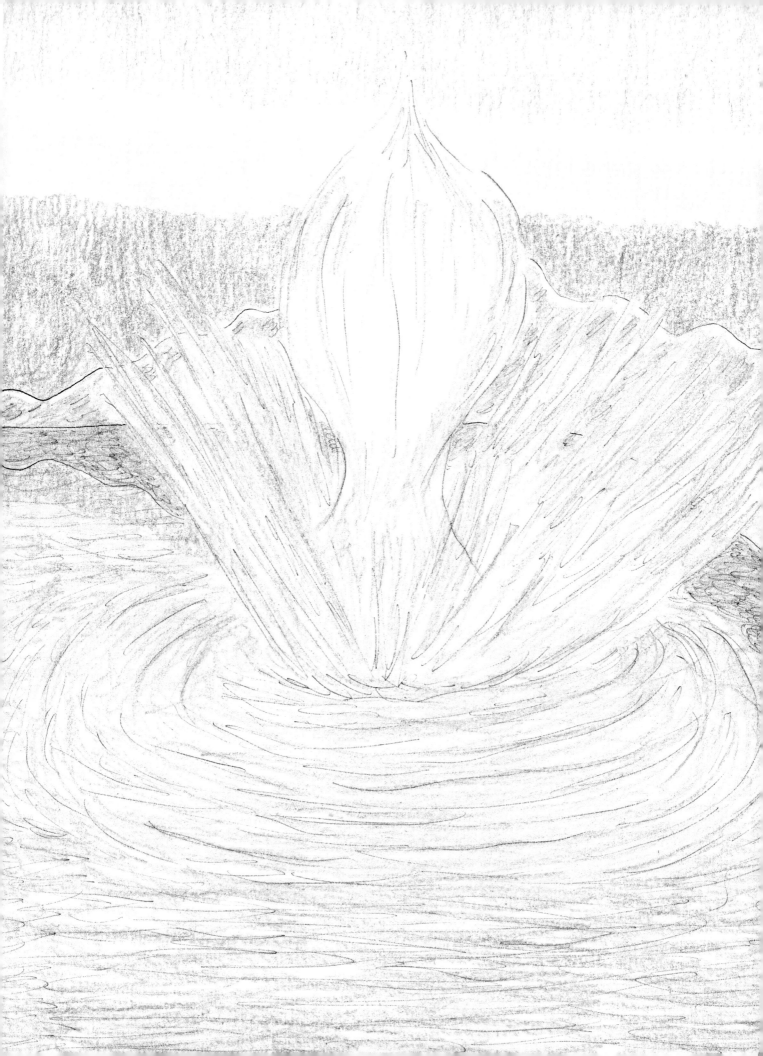

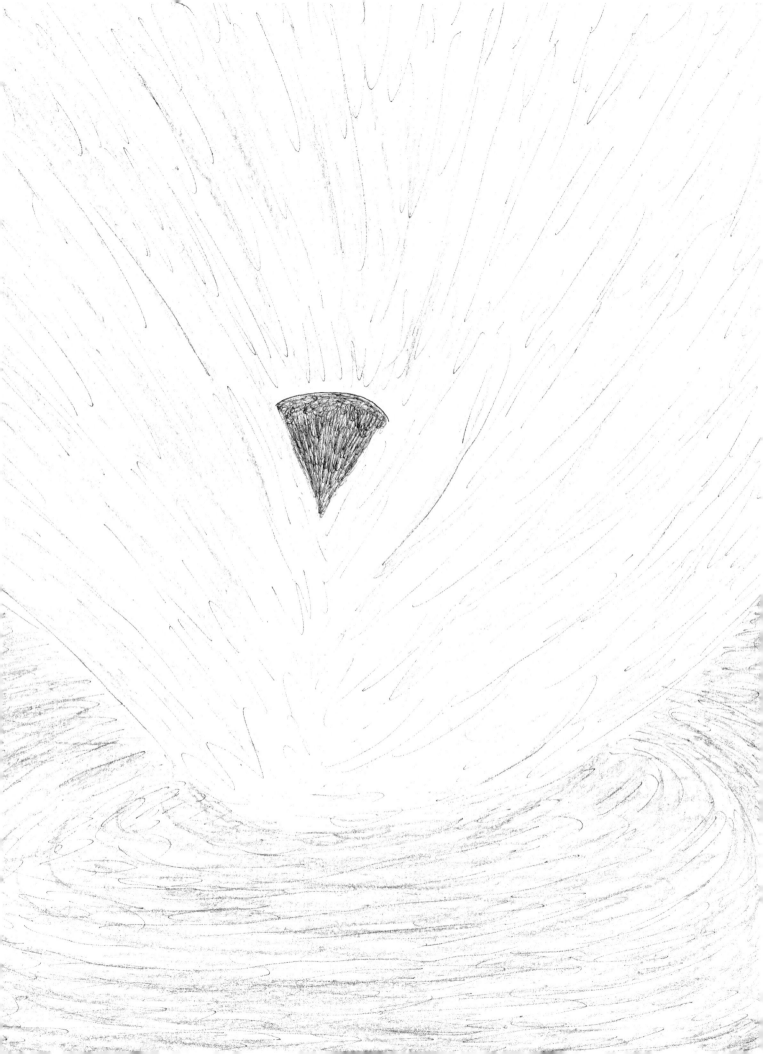

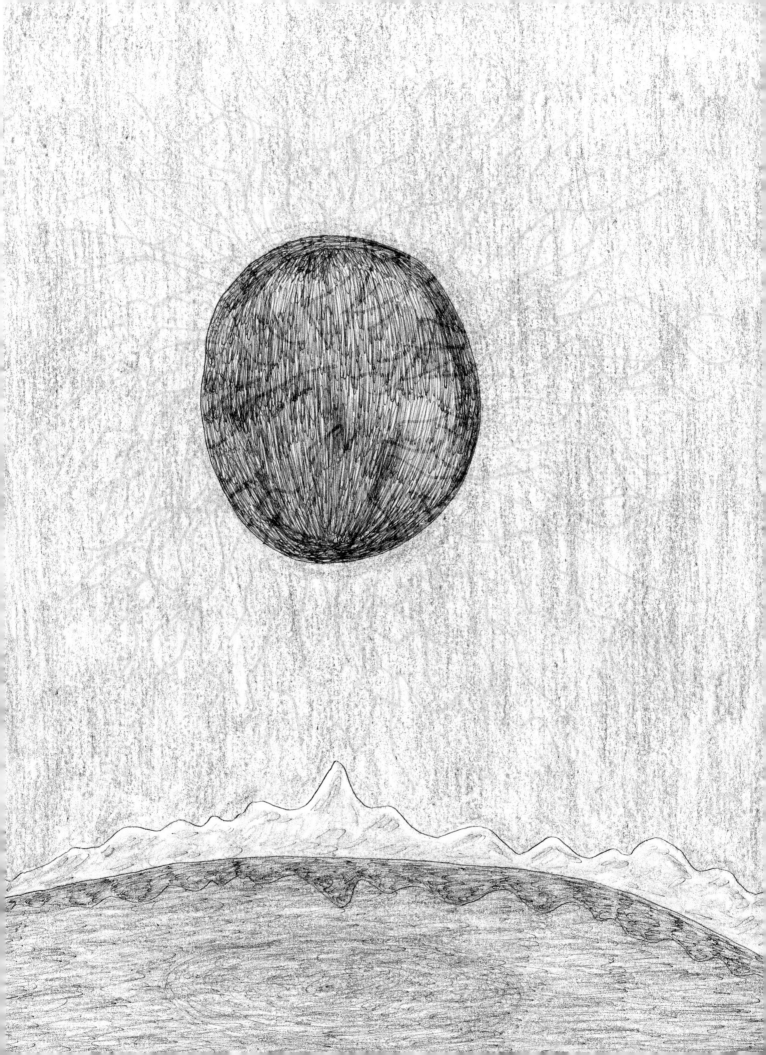

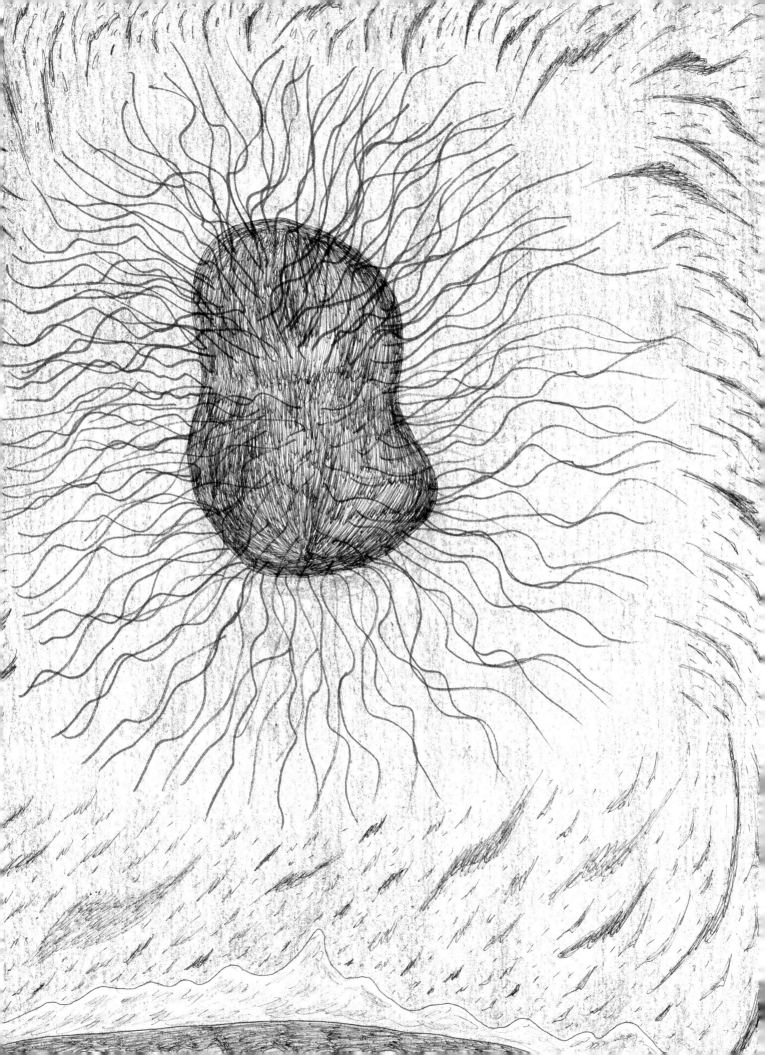

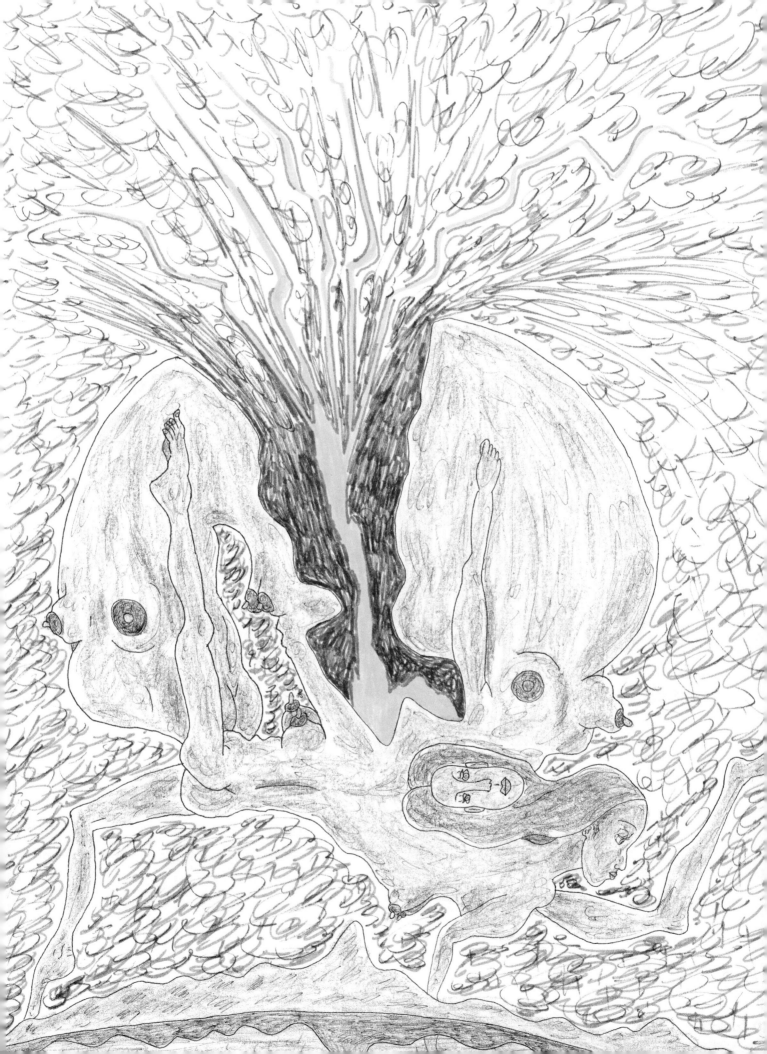

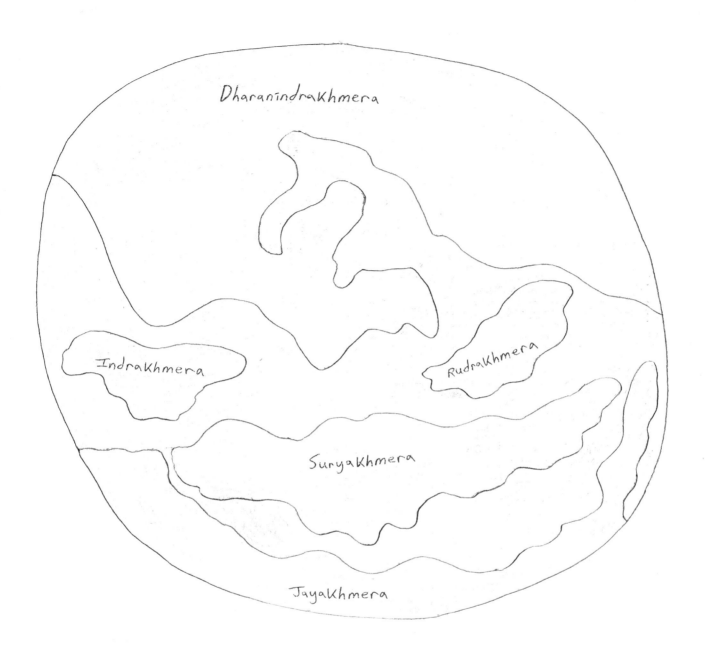

Dharanindrakhmera

Indrakhmera

Rudrakhmera

Suryakhmera

Jayakhmera

WESTERN HEMISPHERE OF
UDAYADITYAKHMERA

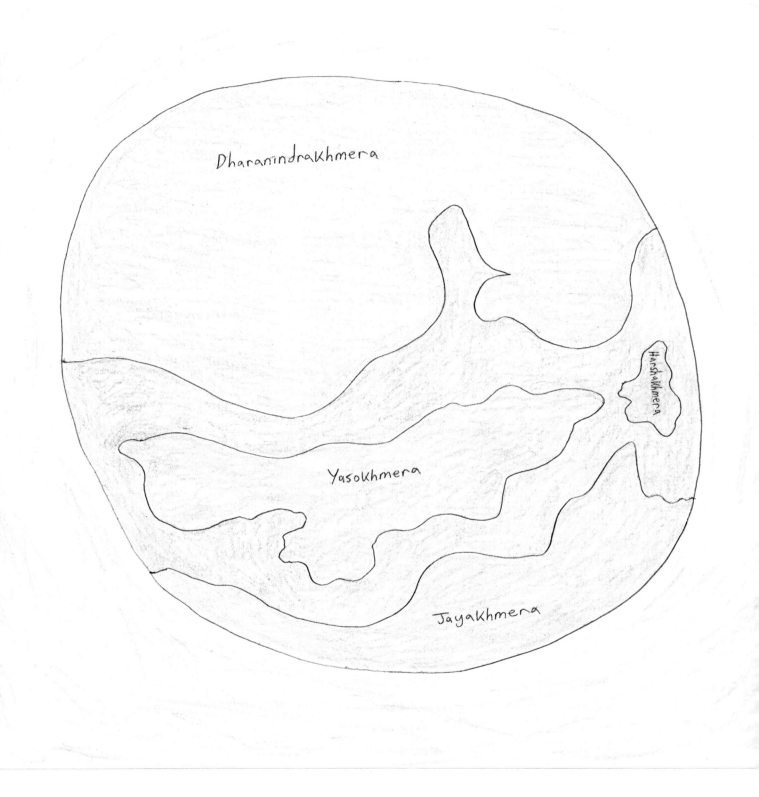

Dharanindrakhmera

Harshakhmera

Yasokhmera

Jayakhmera

EASTERN HEMISPHERE OF
UDAYADITYAKHMERA

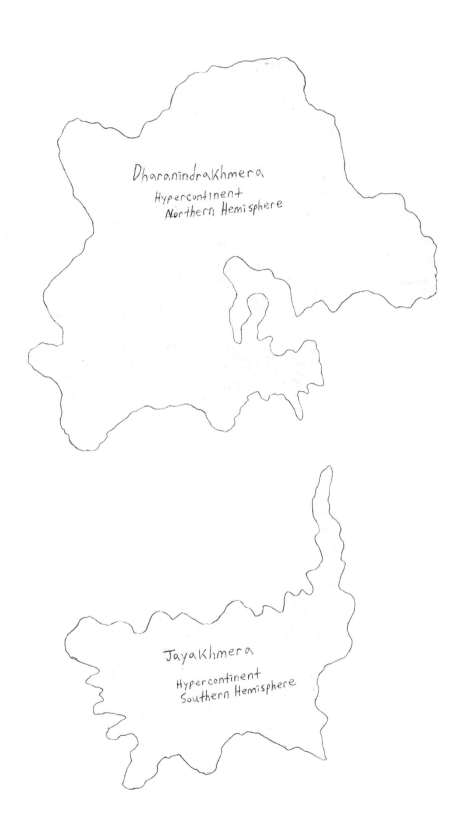

Dharanindrakhmera

Hypercontinent
Northern Hemisphere

Jayakhmera

Hypercontinent
Southern Hemisphere

NORTHERN & SOUTHERN
HEMISPHERE CONTINENTS

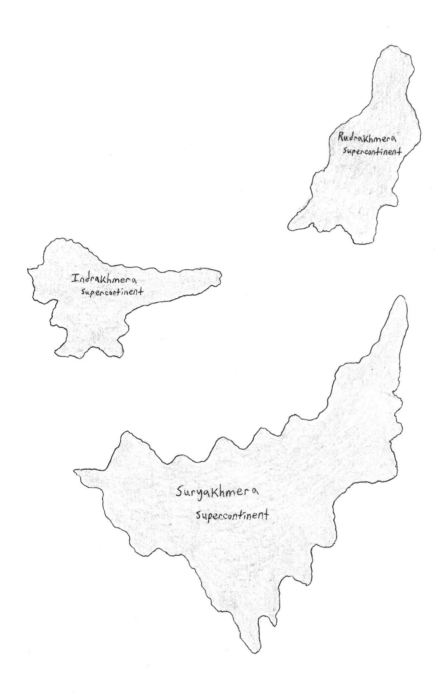

Rudrakhmera
Supercontinent

Indrakhmera
Supercontinent

Suryakhmera
Supercontinent

WESTERN HEMISPHERE CONTINENTS

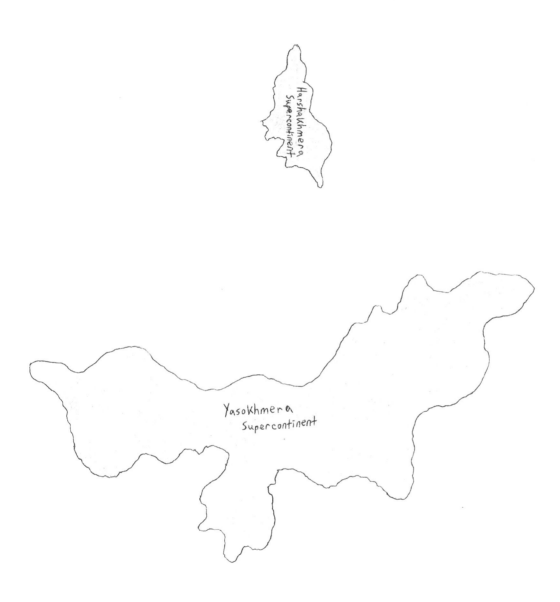

Harshakhmera Supercontinent

Yasokhmera
Supercontinent

EASTERN HEMISPHERE CONTINENTS

Order this book online at www.trafford.com
or email orders@trafford.com

Most Trafford titles are also available at major online book retailers.

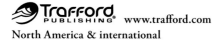 www.trafford.com

North America & international
toll-free: 844 688 6899 (USA & Canada)
fax: 812 355 4082

Our mission is to efficiently provide the world's finest, most comprehensive book publishing service, enabling every author to experience success. To find out how to publish your book, your way, and have it available worldwide, visit us online at www.trafford.com

Because of the dynamic nature of the Internet, any web addresses or links contained in this book may have changed since publication and may no longer be valid. The views expressed in this work are solely those of the author and do not necessarily reflect the views of the publisher, and the publisher hereby disclaims any responsibility for them.

ISBN: 978-1-4269-3243-4 (sc)

Print information available on the last page.

Trafford rev. 02/25/2021